PINKERTON, BEHAVE!
Steven Kellogg

PUFFIN BOOKS

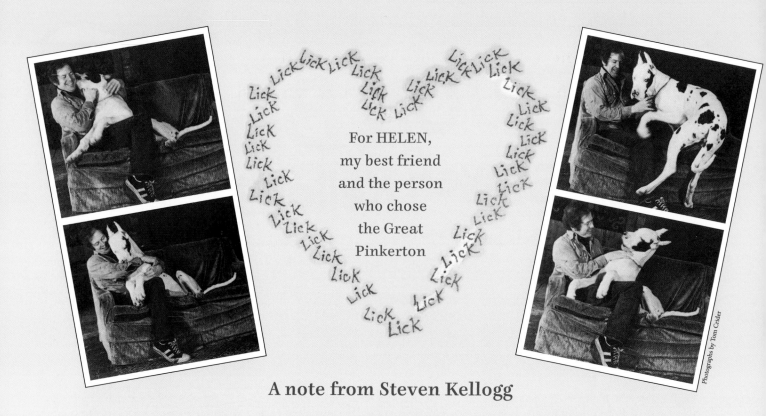

Photographs by Tom Crider

For HELEN,
my best friend
and the person
who chose
the Great
Pinkerton

A note from Steven Kellogg

In this revised edition of *Pinkerton, Behave!* the oversized firearm that was originally included as part of the burglar's stereotyped caricature has been reconsidered and eliminated. This revision in the text and illustrations provided the opportunity to make other adjustments designed to heighten the celebration of the irrepressible Great Dane puppy who brought merriment and chaos into our family during the decade following his arrival in 1976.

PUFFIN BOOKS
An imprint of Penguin Random House LLC
375 Hudson Street · New York, New York 10014

Original edition first published in the United States of America by Dial Books for Young Readers, an imprint of Penguin Random House LLC, 1979
This edition first published Dial Books for Young Readers, 2014
This edition published by Puffin Books, an imprint of Penguin Random House LLC, 2018

Library of Congress Cataloging-in-Publication Data · Kellogg, Steven, author, illustrator. · Pinkerton, behave! / Steven Kellogg.
pages cm · Originally published in 1979. · Summary: "Pinkerton may not be the best-trained dog in his class, but his unconventional behavior saves the day when a burglar comes to his house"— Provided by publisher. · ISBN 978-0-8037-4130-0 (hardcover) · [1. Dogs—Training—Fiction. 2. Behavior—Fiction.] I. Title. · PZ7.K292Pi 2014 · [E]—dc23 · 2013044869 · Manufactured in China on acid-free paper

Puffin Books ISBN 9780451481528

1 3 5 7 9 10 8 6 4 2

Text set in Cosmiqua Com

Every new puppy has to learn to behave.

First I'll teach Pinkerton to come when he's called.

While he's trying to master COME, we'll teach him to FETCH my slippers.

From now on I'll fetch my own slippers.

But it's important for him to defend the house if a burglar shows up.
He'll need to BARK LOUDLY to scare the bad guy away.

I'm afraid Pinkerton needs professional help.
He'll have to go to obedience school.

When this poor creature sees how well my other pupils behave, he will understand what I expect of him.

We begin with the simple command.

We cannot hold back the entire class for one confused student.
ON TO THE NEXT LESSON!

Dogs, PAY ATTENTION!

Our next lesson is a most important one.

Scare away the bad guy!

Your dog's misbehavior sets a poor example for the other students.
Unless he shows immediate improvement, he will be dismissed!

We will now review all that we have learned.

Begin with the simple command.

Mom, you've had a pretty rough day. Why don't you go to bed and get a good night's sleep?

Pleasant dreams, Mom. Pleasant dreams, Pinkerton.

Pinkerton, wake up! It's a bad guy! Scare him away!

Pinkerton, he's a slipper!

Pinkerton, I'm a bad guy.

We love you, Pinkerton.